A

Thimbleful

of Yarns

by

Geoffrey Wilding

With thanks my wife Helen, for excusing me the time spent on the computer, and also to John Charles, for his assistance in checking the prose.

D1826485

Prologue

In early 2018 I joined the Presteigne Writers Circle, which meets monthly, except in December and January.

It has been a rewarding experience to meet other writers and to read and discuss their works.

Over the past months I have presented my offerings to the group, which were generally well received and, rather than leave them to gather dust in a folder, I thought that it might be nice to share them with a wider audience.

As always the title was the first hurdle, what to name a small collection of short stories for a more mature audience, but after several attempts the words 'A Thimbleful of Yarns' coalesced and seemed to sum up this small literary offering perfectly.

Thank you for taking the time to read my work, which I hope you will enjoy.

Other books by Geoff

Imagine – A memoir of Misdiagnosis
(Available from Amazon in Kindle and
paperback formats)

Reprieved – The continuing story of (and
including) Imagine
(Available from Amazon in Kindle and
paperback formats)

Nine Days in Thailand – A memoir of the
Indian Ocean Tsunami
(Available in 2020)

Index

HEAVENS ABOVE!

"What was that!" exclaimed George, coming to with a start "Loud enough to wake the flippin' dead!" he continued grumpily, before remembering, and then realising that he was speaking out loud to himself.

You see there had been a sudden thump on the floor upstairs, a noise loud enough to interrupt George's study of the inside of his eyelids, so loud in fact that it had even penetrated his psyche above the sound of the ballroom dance music, which was emanating from the television. It was Saturday night and 'Strictly' was on, a must see for his late wife Sarah and, although George wasn't that fussed himself, it was one of those comforting, nostalgic, traditions that helped to keep the memory of her alive.

He reached out with his right hand for the remote on the side table, however, his aged dry skin made it slip from his grasp, causing it to rattle further away. "Bugger!" he wheezed. A second attempt though was successful. So purposely reaching forward with the remote cradled in his thin, bony hands, he shakily pointed it at the television and, with an exaggerated up and down movement, he manged to depress the button to mute the sound. "It was probably on too loud anyway," he thought to himself, "Sarah would never have approved"; "Might upset the neighbours," he could hear her say and, as he dropped the remote back onto the table, his eyebrows lifted a little, and a wry smile curled his upper lip.

Determined to find out what had caused the noise, George slapped his hands like grappling irons, one each over the front of the long worn out, threadbare arms of his armchair, and struggled to pull himself forward until he could reach the cross bar of his walker, stationed as it was like a dutiful servant, corralling his knees. His knuckles whitened as he gripped on tightly, enhancing the dull blue colour of the veins under his pallid skin, which was visible from his white knuckles to the frayed cuffs of his burgundy coloured cardigan.
"I can remember when I had muscles," he mused to himself.

With a sharp intake of breath and a loud grunt, George hoisted himself upright, swaying slightly until his blood pressure caught up with his sudden movement. Now steady, he twisted his head slightly, so that his hearing aid microphone pointed squarely at the ceiling, and stood there listening intently for a repetition of the noise, however, none came.

He decided to move further, towards where he thought the noise had come from. He pushed the walker forward, but too late, he looked down and immediately realised that the corduroy slipper, which no longer resided on his left foot, having fallen off while he slept, was now chocking the wheel of the walker, preventing his forward motion. However, the laws of inertia were not to be denied and George, still gripping the walker, fell to the ground with an almighty crash, his head meeting the carpeted floor with a heavy thud, and oblivion ensued.

Mercifully, after a while, George started to rally. At first he thought it must be his eyelids flickering open, but the flashing continued. His next thought was that it must be the telly, but no, hang on a minute, as the haze of unconsciousness started to lift, he could see that the colour of the light was mostly blue and, he could hear voices, which was strange, because he vaguely remembered that he had muted the sound of the television.

George started to stir. "Don't move Sir!" a male voice boomed, closer to his ear than was really comfortable, which startled him, "You've had a fall," he said "Can you tell me your name?"

Beginning to remember recent events George replied "Uh! My name is George; George Turnbull," his voice no more than a dry rattle, from breathing in the dust from the carpet.

"OK George, lay still, I'm just going to check you over," and into George's field of vision came a green clad arm, with a hand covered in wrinkled purple. It started to gently push and prod him.

Next, a young woman with blonde hair, knelt down where he could see her. He noted that she too was clad in green with purple hands, but she also had the added accessory of a yellow dayglo tabard. "Hi George," she said with a soft, warm voice "I need to check your pupils," and she started to flash a pen light in his eyes.

"How did you know to find me?" George croaked, trying to clear his throat.

The young woman replied "The tilt alarm in your walker went off and, when the alarm company couldn't make contact, they alerted us and gave us the key box number, so that we could get in through the front door."

"Oh!" George said simply.

"Do you remember what happened," asked the young woman.

"There was a noise upstairs, and I was trying to find out what it was," George said, now playing the whole memory sequence like a video in his head.

"I'll go and check if you like," said the male paramedic. George couldn't see him, but managed to nod agreement as best he could, and heard a creak as the bulk of the man climbed the stairs.

"Nothing broken," said the young woman reassuringly "Shall we try and get you to sit up?"

"Yes please," said George and, with her help, he managed to twist round and raise himself into a sitting position with his back leaning against the chair.

Within a few minutes a large green and yellow shape appeared at the periphery of George's vision. It was the male paramedic standing in the doorway, who having completed his inspection of the first floor said, "Everything seems secure George. All I could find was this large framed photo of a woman, which seems to have fallen from the wall. It looks like the string broke," and he moved forward, carefully placing the photo frame on George's outstretched legs.

George reached out and lifted it towards him. Tears welled in his eyes and a quivering smile played on his lips.

"Heavens above," he said softly "It's Sarah, she WAS telling me the telly was too loud."

A WORLD OF WHITENESS

A soft glow started to penetrate Brian's closed eyelids, growing second by second in luminosity, focusing his pupils and bringing his rapid eye movement to a stop, interrupting the dream he was having.

Brian opened his eyes, the reflected glow of the concealed lighting having now reached about half of its full intensity, he lifted his left arm so that the back of his forearm shielded his eyes. "Alexa stop!" he called from his prone position, and the lighting level held firm.

As it happens, he wasn't particularly upset that the dream had ended. It hadn't exactly been a nightmare, but it was the third time this week that he'd had to try and extricate himself from a swamp, beating off a few nasty biting things on the way to safety.

"Alexa, what time is it?" Brian quizzed his electronic font of all knowledge. "0700 hours," replied a robotic, though agreeable female voice.
Brian rolled on to his right side, using his elbow to lift his upper torso, he yawned and rubbed his eyes with the back of his left

hand, and then used his fingers to brush and ruffle his dishevelled hair into some semblance of his usual style.

He could see that it must be the weekend, as evinced by the glass and empty wine bottle on the lounge table, clearly visible from his eyrie of a bedroom, up on the mezzanine floor: You see his employers have a very stringent, no alcohol or drugs policy backed up with random testing, which meant this must be a no work day. So why, he puzzled, had he asked 'Alexa' to set the alarm so early.

"Alexa, what's the date?" he said, "The twenty first of December, two thousand and twenty five," came the almost immediate reply.

"Of course," Brian thought "The Winter Equinox."

He pulled back the duvet and swung his legs over the side of the bed. "I don't know what I'd do without you Alexa," he said quietly to himself, so as not to illicit a response.

As he sat on the edge of the bed, trying to control his wayward slippers with his toes, a slight shiver came over him. Brian always had 'Alexa' set the temperature at 18°C at night, which, although not cool, was several degrees lower than he managed to achieve curled up under a 10 tog duvet.

"Alexa, set the temperature to 22°C" he called. Within a few seconds he heard the warm air heating fan click on, so now fully slippered, he made his way to the shower room.

Ablutions soon finished, Brian got dressed in a pair of dark slacks and a white polo shirt, sliding his still bare feet back into his slippers, then, leaning forward in front of the dressing table mirror he picked up the comb and sorted his wayward hair.

"The sun should be rising just about now" he thought, looking at the time on the TV screen, which was integrated into the mirror. It was now five to eight. "Alexa, switch on the TVs," he called, while quickly arranging the pillows and duvet, so as to leave the bed looking tidy for the day, "Alexa, BBC News channel." he added, because it was the only news channel still to run without adverts, even though the 'good ol' Beeb' had finally succumbed, and gone commercial last year.

Brian descended the stairs leading to the kitchenette below. Opening a wall cupboard, he retrieved a box of his favourite coffee cassettes and fitted one into the Tassimo sat on the worktop. He flicked the on switch and, while he waited for the aroma of the newly made coffee, he looked towards the patio doors at the end of the lounge.

The electro- transparency glass was still set at opaque, "Alexa, what's the weather like outside?" he asked.
"The weather in Birmingham today is clear."

"Good," he thought "We should be able to see it then."

The octophonic sound system played the usual pre-recorded chime of notes, heralding the news headlines. The 'News Anchor' read through the bullet points and then handed over to an outside broadcast team, somewhere in the Welsh hills.

"How are things looking where you are Gareth?" he asked.

Gareth smiled to camera and started to read from his iPad. "Alexa, mute" Brian called. He'd been hearing about this for days now and just wanted to drink his coffee in peace.

Although Brian really enjoyed the techno wizardry of having 'Alexa', he wouldn't say that he was a scientifically minded person by any stretch of the imagination. However, he had managed to keep himself abreast of the global warming debate for a number of years now and, to be fair, he had tried hard to listen even handedly, when it came to absorbing the information from both sides of the argument.

He could clearly remember the sharp intake of breath from around the world when, back in 2018, President Trump had pulled

America out of the Paris climate agreement but, in reality, with the millions of people in China and India improving their standard of living and, like Brian, expecting to avail themselves of the trappings of the middle classes; the cars; the electronic devices; the holiday flights overseas etc., the planned reductions in national CO_2 emissions, along with the millions spent on subsidising the renewables sector, had failed to stem the rise in global temperatures.

The latter, he'd understood from the many TV experts, had hastened the melting of the permafrost in the Russian Steppes, releasing millions of metric tons of methane gas into the atmosphere, a greenhouse gas many times more effective than carbon dioxide.

"So here we are as predicted," thought Brian.

Many environmental scientists had forecast that due to the warmer global climate, the earth's atmosphere was becoming super saturated with water vapour, and where moist air met the stratosphere, it would create a permanent layer of cirrostratus [ice particle] cloud. Then what sunlight managed to penetrated this layer would be refracted repeatedly by the water droplets in the low level clouds, before being reflected from the underside of the high level cloud, until this inevitable phenomenon occurred.

They further reasoned that because the air over the industrialised northern hemisphere was more polluted, the effect would be seen here first, before eventually spreading to the entire globe and, the consensus of the various experts was, based on current figures, that it would most likely happen this year or possibly next, when the sun was, as it is now, at its most acute angle.

"The sun must have risen high enough by now," thought Brian, "Alexa, set the windows to clear" he called and, almost immediately, the dull grey of the glass seemed to dissolve. The silhouettes of the neighbouring high rise buildings gradually appeared, as though melding from the slurry of charged lithium crystals, moving within the triple glazing, as their polarity changed.

Picking up his coffee cup, Brian walked towards the patio doors, "Alexa, resume the news" he called, and Gareth's voice resynched with his silent animated portrait.

Brian reached out and slid open the patio doors so that he could step out and get a better view of the sky from his small terrace, some twenty floors above the street below. The orientation of the building meant that the sun was hidden somewhere over his right shoulder, so Brian turned to look in a northerly direction.

"Looks like it's going to be this year then," he said to himself, almost in a whisper, as he lifted the mug to take a comforting sip of coffee on this momentous morning, a day when so much of the sunlight was being trapped in the atmosphere that the sky had turned an eerie monochrome white.

"And there we have it," Gareth announced to the empty lounge, "The first day of many to come in a world of whiteness."

A SENSE OF DUTY

It was late September and Julie was meandering along behind a group of women on a wide, gravel pathway that followed the winding bank of the river Tame as it made its way to the Trent.

It was a bit cooler than it had been of late, but puddles of sunlight frequently warmed the air around her as they made their way across the ground, trying to outpace the pursuing shadows of the flotilla of clouds that sailed effortlessly in the pale blue sky, although not warming her so much that she felt the need to take off her fleece jacket.

Julie's mood was neither happy nor sad, merely contemplatory, as she made her way past the sculpted memorials, each one nestled half hidden in a hewn inlet amid the profusion of trees. Each inlet had a pathway to tempt you to move closer, so as to inspect the inscriptions of valour adorning each plinth.

The fact that Julie was here at the National Memorial Arboretum at all was by pure chance. Her friend Anne, a member of the local WI, had booked and paid for place on this outing but, due to a problem within the family, she had needed to call off, and offered the place to Julie who, although not a member herself, had taken up the offer of a free day out, really just for something to do.

The coach journey had taken all of an hour and a half and, apart from the occasional attempt at inclusion by one or two of the WI ladies from adjoining seats, Julie had spent the time sat by herself watching the world pass by through the large side window, much, she thought to herself, as it had been passing her by for years, completely unhindered by any input on her part to try and alter the situation.

At forty three she was still single, having been the main carer for her enfeebled mother, who had suffered a debilitating stroke while Julie was still in her early twenties. This had proved to be an insurmountable obstacle to Julie pursuing her chosen career as an air hostess and, although her mother had now passed away, Julie's application to several airlines had convinced her that, despite recent changes to legislation, age discrimination was very much alive and kicking. At times of downheartedness on receiving letters of rejection, she was fleetingly rueful of the sense of duty she had felt towards her mother.

Although seemingly not in any particular hurry to keep up with the others, Julie however was on a mission. Anne had asked her, as a favour, to take a couple of photos of the WI memorial, which she thought from her enquiries stood at grid reference G.12 and could be found on the 'Orientation Guide'.

This pamphlet, Anne had neglected to mention, would cost Julie £3 at the reception desk.

She stopped still for a minute and refolded the pamphlet, so that the side bearing the map was uppermost and rested it on the palm of her left hand then. She traced along the grid references with her right forefinger, "Must be about here somewhere," she thought to herself and looking up she saw off to her left a low level, 'S' shaped, dry stone wall with an integral stone bench, almost like a tête-à-tête sofa.

A little dubious as to whether this was indeed the right memorial, Julie stepped onto the grass and walked over to check it out. As she got nearer, she could see that the curved shape stood on two circles of irregular shaped stone slabs, each with a central circular stone, which had been inscribed with the tree emblem of the WI, although the weather and footfall had worn most of the accompanying wording away.

Having established that this was the right place, she stepped back and took several photos from different angles, using the camera on her smart phone. Pleased that she had fulfilled Anne's request, she walked back to the path and started to make her way towards the Remembrance Centre at the entrance, as it was near the time she had been told to assemble for refreshments and then wait for the coach to take everyone back home.

After about 100 yards or so, Julie's attention was drawn to another memorial. It was far more intricate than the one she had just photographed, being in the shape of a tree with outstretched branches supported on a fence of open diagonal wooden slats. Intrigued, Julie made her way to the opening in the surrounding timber fence and walked inside.

The patination of the tree, located in the centre of the space, suggested to her that it was probably cast out of bronze and, now that she was closer, she could see that pieces of weathered copper sheet in the shape of leaves had been hung from small bronze eyelets under the branches, each one suspended by a small split ring, the sort that are used on key fobs. Then, looking down, she noticed that a brass plaque had been secured to the base of the tree, inscribed with the parent's grieving sentiments to an eight year old boy who had passed away some ten years previously.

A slight breeze picked up and the leaves started to flutter, as though about to fall in a perpetual autumn. Julie looked closer at the dancing leaves and could see that on some of them, the rusted steel split rings had worn the copper leaves away to such an extent that they were actually close to falling off for real.

"I'm sure they wouldn't miss just one if I took it as a memento of the day," she thought to herself, particularly as money was always tight these days and, all the items she had looked at earlier in the gift shop were quite expensive.

Julie glanced furtively around and, when she was sure that she could not be seen, she reached up and plucked one of the more fragile leaves from the tree, sneaking it into her shoulder bag, quickly closing the flap, allowing herself a secret smile on the success of operation 'falling leaf'.

As Julie turned to leave with her souvenir, her smile quickly faded, immediately replaced with a hot flush of embarrassment, which rose inexorably through her cheeks, causing a tingling sensation at the tops of her rapidly reddening ears.

There, in front of her, adjacent to the opening in the wooden fence was something previously unseen. Fixed to the wall, no doubt purposely at eye level, was a small black painted box with a slit in the front. A white notice with black writing sat above it, a motionless challenge, clearly stating that if anyone found a fallen leaf they should place it in the box, so that it could be rehung and thereby the memorial maintained for future generations.

Julie felt her heart in her throat and her mouth suddenly went dry, as though she had sucked on a lemon. She re-read the notice, her hand clenched tightly onto the repository of the proceeds of her wrongdoing, and an all-consuming guilt rooted her to the spot.

Then slowly, the same sense of duty, which she had once shown to her mother, came to the fore and reassigned itself to the memory of the lost child, the parents that grieved for him, the artist who had crafted the memorial and to those who look after it.

Almost in slow motion, her hand moved to lift the flap of her shoulder bag and retrieve the 'fallen' leaf. She then reached purposefully forward, and placed the origin of her feeling of unworthiness into the box. The sense of relief she felt at the sound of the leaf hitting the bottom of the box was palpable.

Julie then stepped through the opening in the fence, quickly looking both ways, as though checking to see if her shortcoming had been noticed. She moved hurriedly along the intersecting pathways, never once looking back, trying to make it to the Remembrance Centre by the shortest route possible and, once there, she made for the group of WI ladies, who, after having enjoyed their tea and cakes, had now gathered, chatting in the foyer, waiting for the coach to swing into view across the glass frontage.

"You've missed the refreshments I'm afraid," said the group leader to Julie "Have you enjoyed your day?"

Julie, still somewhat short of breath from her exertions, smiled weakly at her and said "I think I've come to fully understand what a sense of duty means."

The group leader nodded back and smiled.

THE SEQUENCE OF SEASONS

Ryan, a tall, sinewy, Afro-American, paced nervously around a short elliptical course, glancing at the pair of computer screens on his desk at each revolution. He could feel the eyes of his colleagues almost burning into him.

Gary, his stockily built friend and work colleague of the past two years was sat, arms folded, in Ryan's chair, also glued to the screens. He turned and looked over his shoulder at Ryan. "Calm down Bud, you won't make it happen any quicker by wearing a hole in the floor," he said, trying to ease the obvious tension of his friend.

Ryan stopped and with both hands leaned heavily on the back of the chair. He peered down over Gary's mop of ginger hair, his eyes darting between the bottom right hand corners of both screens "Two minutes thirty and counting," he said intently, as if willing the flickering numbered countdown to speed to a conclusion.

Ryan and Gary had both started working for NOAA (*The National Oceanic and Atmosphere Administration*) within a couple of weeks of each other at their National Severe Storms Laboratory in Norman, Oklahoma.

Ryan had worked his way through Alabama State University, having achieved a sports scholarship in basketball, eventually distinguishing himself playing for the Hornets. Gary, on the other hand, had studiously made his way through Harvard; however, being a keen follower of his home team, the Philadelphia 76ers, he and Ryan had soon struck up a friendship based on their common interest in basketball, making for several beer fuelled, and sometimes heated, although always friendly, discussions on the NBA rankings.

The cause of Ryan's obvious agitation had occurred the day before. He had recently been working, with Gary and the others, on a joint project to try and establish the effects of 'Global Warming' weather patterns, in particular, on how they might affect American farmers with seasonal crop growing.

His input to the project was to try and forecast what part the high level 'Jet Streams' would play and, over the two days previous, he had, or at least he thought he had, diligently keyed in the received data from the research stations around the world, before pressing the 'Enter' key to start the computation process. Even with the massive racks of processors available at NOAA, the trillions of binary code switches necessary for the calculation would still take about ten hours to churn out the result so, feeling quite happy that his work was done, he had gone home in a relaxed mood.

Keen to know the outcome of his toils, he had returned to work at around 08.30hrs yesterday, but, seeing that the screens were still showing the final calculation countdown, he had chivvied Gary from his desk to go and grab a coffee with him, and discuss the pros and cons of last night's televised basketball game.

The banter continued between them as Ryan returned to his desk, coffee in hand. He was still facing Gary's workstation, riposting an incoming jibe, as he reached for his office chair, turning to look at the screens as he started to sit down.

The surprise at what he saw caused him to misjudge the chair's position, making it swivel sideways on its castors, tipping him and his coffee onto the floor.

Gary's initial reaction was one of hilarity. "I wish I'd got that on my phone for a YouTube post," he called but, on seeing Ryan crawl forward on his knees, grabbing hold of the edge of the desk for support, absorbed totally by what he was looking at, Gary quickly made his way to his friend's side, where he too became transfixed by the images before him.

"I thought you were calculating 'Jet Steam' circulations" he said.

"I am …… I mean I did," Ryan replied somewhat obliquely, his gaze still mesmerized by what he was looking at.

Alerted by the crash of the chair, a group of work colleagues had now started to gather in Ryan's work area, each one carefully avoiding the puddle of coffee, which had now expanded to the full extent that its viscosity would allow. "I'll get some paper and clear that up," said one of them, which received a mutual murmur of thanks from the others, who were now fully engrossed in the situation.

The left hand screen showed graph lines of differing colours rising from a midpoint on the left side and rising at various divergent angles as they traversed to the right, a couple of which disappeared off the top of the screen long before arriving. However, it was the right hand screen which held everyone's attention. In the centre was a large circle across which were several horizontal bands of colour, ranging from red at the middle through shades of orange, finishing with a yellow skullcap section at the top and bottom.

"So what does this one show?" enquired Gary further, pointing at the right hand screen, trying to assimilate the straight bands with what he knew should be the undulating lines of the 'Jet Stream', forming the high and low pressure areas that create the ground level weather.

Ryan, struggling to regain some control of the situation and, realising that this was his work and that all eyes were now upon him, "Ah! ..... Well! From the figures," he stammered, turning to his audience, while at the same time pointing at the relevant spot on the screen "It would appear that they relate to alternating bands of wind circling the planet."

"What, a bit like Jupiter?" someone asked.

"Sort of," said Ryan, trying to sound more sure than he actually was.

"Looks a bit more like 'fat finger' entries to me" came the unhelpful reply from another in the audience, which heralded some knowing chuckles.

His gathered colleagues then seemed to part from the rear, and Professor Clancy squeezed her way through to stand next to Ryan; not that easy for a woman of her ample proportions, which had no doubt been gained from years of siting at a desk, while she worked through her empirical thesis on weather systems. It had been a stunning piece of work that had gained many plaudits, eventually leading to her current prestigious role at NOAA.

"What seems to be the problem Ryan?"

"Well Jean," started Ryan "The latest set of results seem to have thrown up a bit of a 'Jet Stream' enigma."

"So what is it we are looking at?" she questioned, looking directly at Ryan and then back at the screen.
"It would seem, if the figures are correct, that by the year 2099 there will no longer be the 'Jet Stream' as we know it, but rather this striated pattern of winds." Ryan, trying to find the relevant figure on the screen and then, pointing at it, continued "With maintained equatorial wind speeds of 200 plus miles per hour at ground level." A high pitched, though soft, whistle emanated from someone in the audience.

"How many times have you run the programme?" asked Professor Clancy.

"Just the once so far," replied Ryan.

"Has any of the data inputs from the research centres changed dramatically?" she added.

"Not really," replied Ryan, then recalling, he added "Except …… that the new information from NASA's Parker Solar Probe was included for the first time in the programme update last month."

"Right then," said Professor Clancy, quickly thinking what to do next. "Well, before I take this forward you will need to run the programme again" then asked "Gary, are you able to give Ryan a hand without disruption to your project?"

"No problem Jean," replied Gary.

"OK then, the show's over for the moment. Can you guys give Ryan and Gary some space – Thankyou everyone," and with that the audience melted back into their various work stations. "We'll speak again in the morning," Professor Clancy said, and left them to get on with what everyone knew would be a long slog.

Ryan and Gary had worked late and, after checking and rechecking each other's work, and had finally pressed the 'Enter' key at around 22.30hrs, long after everyone else had gone home. This had meant a rather prolonged, meticulous exit through security. However, after what had been a fairly sleepless night, here they were again this morning, waiting for the computer to finish its labours.

Ryan watched as Professor Clancy made her way towards his desk, with other colleagues from the office falling in behind her, eager to know the outcome.

"How's it going?" she asked Ryan

"Only seconds to go," answered Gary.

There was a sense of expectation from the gathered audience as the on screen timer sped towards zeros. The screens blanked for a brief moment before defiantly displaying the same two images they had the day before.

"Shit!" someone exhaled, which seemed to sum up the conversion of those that had previously been sceptical.

"OK!" Professor Clancy said, turning with her back to the desk having quickly understood the gravity of the situation. "Two things people," she continued, "One! This has to stay in house until I say otherwise," which garnered a wide eyed stare from some, but more generally, a knowing muttering of agreement. "…….. And the second is," she said, pausing so that she had full attention once more "The emphasis of this department will now have to change, and be on how this new information affects all the programmes we are working on at this time."

"Sort of makes my work on the sequence of seasons a bit irrelevant," offered Gary, ironically.

Brushing aside his friend's comment Ryan asked "But what's caused it Jean?" putting voice to a question that was now at the forefront of everyone's mind.

"Well, I did some work on this myself last night," she replied "and it seems that the Parker Solar Probe has found that our sun is expanding earlier in its life cycle than had been anticipated, which has led to an increase in the influence of the solar wind.

"Ah!" Interrupted Ryan "That might explain the reports we've been receiving from our polar research stations over the past couple of years, about the exceptionally vibrant Aroura they've been recording."

"Quite possibly Ryan," said Professor Clancy, turning to him and acknowledging his input with a nod. "Anyway," she continued "In time, the more energetic solar wind will start to impact on the poles, a bit like a duvet cover, which will reduce any heat loss that is presently gained from the seasonal tilting of the planet.

The effect will be to significantly reduce the current variations between the temperatures at the poles and the equator, to such an extent that the 'Jet Stream' fluctuations will become less and less dynamic, until eventually the atmosphere is spun into the banding pattern shown in Ryan's computer model."

The shock of this revelation hitting home on the psyche of her captive audience was almost audible.

"That'll be a global catastrophe." A statement voiced by one, but thought by everyone.

"Well it certainly focuses the mind," replied Professor Clancy, trying to reign in her own thoughts that were already racing towards unthinkable conclusions

"So now, as I said earlier, please reassess your programmes and let me have your thoughts by the end of the day, while, in the meantime, I have to go and speak to someone at the White House"

With that Jean turned and walked briskly back to her office, inwardly struggling with the enormity of the statement she was about to make; while Ryan stood with Gary staring at the screens, the yet untold tragedy of the images taking away any thought of speaking.

A KEEN SENSE OF THE MOMENT

First a loud crash!! Then, "Get off of me Peter!" followed closely by Ollie's tears.

Bill looked up from the newspaper that was spread on the kitchen table, and put down his half empty mug of now tepid tea, probably a little more forcibly than he should have, because now a light brown stain was expanding on the page he had been reading.

"Here we go!" Bill said rhetorically to Ethel, who was standing at the kitchen sink with a plate and tea towel in hand, finishing the last of the lunch time washing up.

"Your turn, I'm busy," Ethel replied, reaching up and placing the now dry plate, with a clatter, on top of the pile in the open cupboard over sink.

It was the school holidays and, as had become usual at this time of year, Bill and Ethel, although probably Ethel more than Bill, had agreed to look after their two grandsons, Peter 9 and Ollie 8, so that their daughter Sarah could continue her part time office job through the summer.

The recession had put a lot of financial pressure on both her and son-in-law James and, although adequate, Bill and Ethel's pensions were not of the order that could allow them to act as the 'Bank of Mum & Dad', well, not without jeopardising their own hard worked for standard of living anyway. So although somewhat tiring at times, it really was the only solution.

"That's what families are for," was the stock answer Ethel trotted out, whenever Sarah asked if they were sure they were alright still doing the childminding.

Bill grabbed the back of the chair he was sitting on, gripping it tightly with his right hand, and placed his left palm flat on the table. He strove to lift himself upwards, the strength of his thigh muscles endeavouring to raise his portly frame against the forces of gravity, particularly as his dodgy knees were operating about as smoothly as a couple of rusty, medieval door hinges.

He turned and took a short pace towards the door before letting go of the support provided by the back of the chair.

"I'll be back," he said to Ethel, with as best an 'Arnie' accent as he could muster.

"You've got to get there first," she replied, her face breaking into the loving smile, the one that had first captured his heart all those years ago.

Bill smiled back resignedly, and nodded in silent agreement.

As he navigated the short distance from the kitchen to the door which led from the hall into the lounge, Bill called out "Right you two, pack it in, whatever you're doing," expecting that the tone of his voice alone would bring peace and tranquillity.

Fat chance!

On entering the room he could see that the cause of the crash had been the side table to the sofa, now skewed on its side, still propped off of the floor slightly by the TV magazines and box of tissues that normally adorned it. On the sofa, a squirming heap of contorted limbs, with Ollie on his back, his arm at full stretch, pushing up under Peter's chin as hard as he could, trying to keep him at bay and Peter bearing down on Ollie's chest with his left forearm, while trying to dislodge Ollie's counter move with his right.

"Oi! I said pack it in you two! Are you two deaf or something?" Bill asked, his voice now raised a notch or two, trying to be more persuasive, but with limited success.

"He started it!" Ollie strained to say through gritted teeth.

"No I didn't," Peter countered, with difficulty, his jaw somewhat immobilised by Ollie's outstretched arm.

"You kicked me you dipstick!" said Peter.

"Liar!" Ollie retorted.

"Enough! The pair of you," chided Bill and, reaching down, he took hold of Peter's right ear and Ollie's left ear, each between a pinching forefinger and thumb, something which their sudden change of facial expression showed was not at all what they were expecting.

"Ow!" they said in unison, "That hurts Granddad."

"Well stop when I tell you to," Bill said, relieved that he had at last managed to bring some order to the chaos and, still holding onto their sensitive appendages, he guided them to their feet. "You shouldn't be fighting" Bill admonished them.

Peter being the elder, and far more precocious than Ollie said in disgruntled tones, "I bet you fought when you were our age."

"Did you Granddad?" chimed Ollie, somewhat brighter, now separated from his tormentor.

Bill paused and, in that instant, his thoughts were transported back to a time, not long after the Second World War, when life was much different. He would have been about Peter's age, but nowhere near as forward.

It was a much simpler time, when boys could be boys and girls were still alien beings that wandered around pushing dolls prams, or playing at skipping.

Happiness could be had by racing carts made from orange boxes and old bike wheels, or with your mates, naively charging up and down the alleyways behind the houses, arms out wide, screaming "Neeeeow" and "Dukkha! Dukkha! Dukkha!" before exclaiming "Gotcha!" when you felt that you had downed one of them.

He hadn't really understood that his sole existence was due to the fortunate happenstance of his father having survived such conflicts, nor was it talked about, either at home or at play.

It was at this time that he had physically needed to defend himself, in fact the only time.

As with all avenues in life, you can't please everyone, and a lad called Roberts, the school bully, had taken a serious dislike to Bill, although quite why, he had no idea.

At first Bill had tried to appease him but, when this had failed he avoided him as much as possible, which had for a while kept a lid on the situation, but there was this one day.

Bill lived close enough to the school to go home for lunch, so he would leave the school gate at the sound of the lunchtime bell and wander through the age grimed, brick wall lined alleyways, back home to where his mum would always have something scrummy for him to eat.

He was not far from home this particular day, when Roberts, closely followed by Fletcher, his ally and near permanent shadow, stepped out from a hidden recess in a garden wall and blocked his path.

At first Bill, thinking of the pain and blood that might flow, gave thought to flee, but quickly concluded that the pair of them would only chase after him, so he stood his ground.

Then Roberts, with Fletcher following close behind, started towards him calling him names and threatening to punch his lights out.

Bill had a sudden urge to pee, but just knew that he mustn't, after all, a black eye was one thing, but he would never be able face down the name calling that would befall him if Roberts could say, with Fletcher's backing, that Bill had wet himself, because he was scared.

Bill decided that his best move was to back up to the nearest wall and wait, then at least no one could get behind him.

As Roberts got close he lunged at Bill, throwing a punch, which landed fairly meekly on his chest. Bill dropped his satchel so that he had both hands free. Roberts lunged again, this time with a lower punch, however, before it made contact Bill managed to grab Roberts' arm at the wrist and turned so that his back was to his assailant. Roberts, unable to halt his forward motion, banged his nose hard on the back of Bill's head making a cracking sound as it hit. Bill felt some pain, but it was Roberts who let out the scream.

Then, with a keen sense of the moment, Bill, who still had his back to Roberts, and had managed to maintain a tight grip on his assailant's arm, realised that he needed to finish this here and now, or he would likely suffer further assaults in the future.

So, pulling forward, he pushed Roberts's clenched fist hard into the brick wall, and rubbed it from side to side.

Roberts screamed as his knuckles were grazed and, taking his other hand from his bloody nose, pushed against Bill's back, trying to regain his damaged hand from Bill's grasp.

He screamed again, this time at Fletcher, "Get him of! Get him off!" at which point Bill released Roberts's arm and turned to face Fletcher, who quickly decided to stop where he was.

Roberts, now holding his right arm up at shoulder height using his left hand, staggered backwards, almost falling into Fletcher's arms "You bastard!" he shouted at Bill.

"You started it!" retorted Bill, his muscles shivering from the adrenalin overload, as he reached down to gather up his satchel.

Roberts and Fetcher turned and walked away, and in the years of schooling that followed, Roberts had never bothered Bill again.

Having come to the lounge door to see what had happened, Ethel took up the boy's question, her voice tearing Bill from his reverie "Well did you Granddad?" she asked "Answer the boys."

Bill quickly repacked his boyhood secret and said rather too haughtily, and with a slight reddening of the cheeks, "No! Of course not"

"Come on," said Ethel, smiling to the boys, "Let's get this mess cleaned up before your Mum gets here."

NOTHING IS CERTAIN UNTIL IT HAPPENS

Professor Pierre Bessette, a middle aged French Biologist, his hair greying at the temples who, although smartly attired, had loosened his tie and undone the top button of his shirt.

He stood rubbing his chin with his right hand, while looking with an unseeing stare out of his office window, situated as it was on the seventh floor of the WHO Headquarters building in Geneva. Thin shards of sunlight pierced the dark clouds that were gathering overhead, much like the political storm of blame now brewing amongst the capitals of the world.

The question that was exercising his every thought at this moment was whether this could be the start of the long expected pandemic, the one prophesised by many health experts over a number of years, but which luckily, until now anyway, had never materialised.

At one time it was thought that avian flu might be the curtailer of the human race but, if the information he had just studied on his computer screen was correct, this threat was much worse, certainly many times more so than the 'Spanish Flu' that had killed 100 million after the first World War, and which might even be unstoppable.

He was so absorbed in thought that he jumped slightly at the knock on his door. "Come!" he called, quickly turning and taking a few steps across the room to meet the cause of the diversion "Have you got the figures Gail?" he said, reaching forward to take the hastily proffered sheets of paper, the contents of which Pierre was already scanning as he turned towards his desk.

Dr Gail Edwards was a researcher allocated to Pierre's office. She was a bespectacled young woman who liked to wear her blonde hair tied back in a ponytail; she was wearing a floral blouse with a black skirt and flat pumps, the latter she wore to belie her tall stature, but which today were proving very well suited for the amount of fetching and carrying she was having to do.

"As we thought Gail," Pierre said, intently studying the papers a sheet at a time, "Most of the coastal areas around the Pacific rim." "It certainly looks that way Professor," she replied, mirroring the look of concern now creasing Pierre's forehead. "Over recent months there have been many reports of huge shoals of dead fish and flocks of dead seabirds, floating on the surface in several areas, as well as beachings of whole pods of dolphin, whale and porpoise."

"Yes" Pierre replied distractedly, still engrossed with the figures, then looking directly at Gail "….. and now coastal towns and villages are reporting people dying in significant numbers from extremely virulent cholera type symptoms, with most of them dead within only a few hours of the first signs of illness."

"If you go to page five," Gail offered, walking towards Pierre's desk, pointing at the relevant page "It shows that autopsy results from the fish, birds and mammals have shown lethal levels of bacterial infection, which have tested to be antibiotic resistant."

"Mon Dieu!" Pierre uttered, his native tongue best expressing his unease, "It now seems to be trans-species as well." Research in the past eighteen months had shown that plastics, far from being impervious, actually have a striated micro surface which, in the right conditions, is well suited for encouraging bacterial growth.

The recent public clamour for action regarding the amount of plastics harming sea creatures, had highlighted the fact that many of the world's largest rivers were the source, annually sluicing millions of tons of waste plastic into the oceans, which over many years had formed great areas known as 'garbage patches'.

This waste plastic had spent a long time migrating down rivers that in some cases are little more than open sewers. Being constantly immersed in a soup of excreted bacterial infection, assisted by warm wet conditions, allowed the bacteria to multiply exponentially and evolve into more lethal strains. Added to this the worldwide explosion in the manufacture and ingestion of antibiotics, a lot of which pass straight through digestive tract, means that the plastic borne bacteria had also been exposed to many of the current antibiotics, allowing them to become totally resistant.

"The link is right there," Pierre said, gesturing at the pages on his desk "The fish and birds ingest the plastic and those not killed as a direct result, are finished off by the toxins exuded by the bacteria plus, somewhere along that timeline, many of the fish are caught and eaten by the coastal communities, and they too are now dying from disease caused by these antibiotic resistant bacteria."

"The rate of spread of disease has been phenomenal" Gail added

"I know, frighteningly so," Pierre responded "…… and, as people become carriers and travel, it won't be long before this becomes an inland problem as well."

"Is there anything that can be done?" Gail asked with a note of anxiety in her voice.

Pierre, with both arms now at full stretch supporting his sagging upper body on his desk, looked up at Gail "Nothing is certain until it happens Gail, but it will be impossible to clean up the oceans quick enough to deal with the problem, and the pathogen is already well established in the human population. It has all the required elements necessary to create a worldwide Pandemic. The best that can happen is that either the drug companies quickly find a hitherto unknown antigen or, failing that, we can only hope that some people prove to have a natural immunity and through them the human race survives."

Pierre gathered the papers together, tapped them on the desk and secured them in a folder, which he then laid on the desk. He lifted his chin so that he could do up his collar and tighten his tie. Walking to the coat stand to collect his jacket, he turned to Gail and said "Are you coming?"

"Where?" she replied

Pierre returned to collect the folder from his desk.

"To tell the world," he said, a disconsolate expression signalling his resignation to the facts.

AN UNANSWERED QUESTION

Great Aunt Flo was a short, jolly soul, nearly as round as she was tall, who had lived in the same small terraced house where she had been born in the latter years of the 1800s. She spoke with a lovely Dorset accent and had a mop of silvery hair that had never passed a hair dresser's threshold.

Her National Health glasses, were always perched on her button nose, with the curly wire arms tucked behind her ears. However, the most memorable thing about Great Aunt Flo, apart that is from the random whiskers on her chin, was that her house was always full of the sweet aroma of baking; cakes mostly.

Once, or sometimes twice a year, we four children would be packed into the family charabanc and taken by mum and dad on the three hour [depending on traffic] journey to see her. When we arrived, all 'at their wits-end' parents, and 'fed-up' children, she would come to the door and welcome us warmly with her usual, almost rhetorical "Come in," "Lovely to see you," "How was the journey," "I'll put the kettle on," never pausing for breath for anyone to answer in between.

We would then have to wait while she did a bobbly pirouette, and lead the way through the narrow hallway to the parlour, her rotund frame acting like a rolling 'road block' to even the smallest sibling who dared to try to overtake her.

It almost felt like we were being sucked towards the parlour, with Great Aunt Flo huffing and puffing her bulk along at the front, creating a virtual vacuum in her wake.

As she passed through the doorway into the parlour and then on to the kitchen beyond, it was as if the vacuum dissipated and we were propelled forward into the spaces between the furniture.

"Orange squash for the children please Flo," mum always reminded her.

"I think I've got some in the larder somewhere," would inevitably come the reply, above the sound of her aged, trembling hands, rattling china cups onto very forgiving saucers.

Even when the sun was out, I remember the parlour being quite a small, dark, fussy room, with numerous small picture frames hung haphazardly on the walls and deep red velvet curtains drawn back at the window, revealing heavily patterned, off white nets through which you could just make out the rollers of a large, old fashioned, laundry mangle in the courtyard.

A small oval table with its opened leaves, supported on fold out legs, and corralled by four ladder back mahogany dining chairs, stood in the corner of the room under the window, patiently waiting to be called into service.

This left just enough room for a tall, blue and white crockery bedecked, open top dresser, and a small, two seater settee with matching arm chair, both upholstered in a faded, jacquard fabric and having antimacassars on the backs and arms which, when moved, would reveal the secret of the original colour of the fabric.

But, none of this was of concern when we children were sat at the table confronted with a glass of orange squash, and a large slice of Great Aunt Flo's still warm, straight from the cooling tray, jam filled Victoria sponge.

It's amazing how the smell of something can transport you to another place and time. All these memories had come flooding back to me when my wife asked me to try a slice of her jam filled, Victoria sponge, the first thing she had baked in her newly installed oven.

"You can only properly test a new oven by baking a Victoria sponge," she said "So let me know what you think?"

As I tucked into the still slightly warm confection, my thoughts once again drifted back to Great Aunt Flo's parlour, as if I was sitting at the small round table, drinking squash and eating cake, and I could still envision the cast iron fire surround, with the well-polished, silver picture fame standing on the mantle shelf.

It held an old, faded, black and white photograph of a man, dressed in First World War army uniform and, under the glass, it had a strip of black ribbon set diagonally across one corner.

As a child I used to wonder who the person in the photograph was, but never found the nerve to ask and now, in this 100th year of commemoration, I really wanted to know his story but, as with the photo itself, all who could tell me were long gone.

A familiar voice came crashing into the echo from my past "Well, what do you think of the sponge?"

"Ah! Lovely dear," I said, licking the last of the icing sugar from my lips "I can't wait for the next offering from your new oven."

It's never a bad thing to earn a few brownie points along the way.

DOCTORS AND NURSES

The evidences of the Second World War were diminishing, and I, the eldest of four siblings; me, my sister and then two younger brothers were, at the time of this story, living with our parents in a large, semi-detached, between the wars built house, which had a neatly tended, and gated front garden that faced onto the main arterial route into the town centre. I must have been about nine or ten, so my sister would have probably been eight, coming on nine, as her birthday was before mine.

Beyond the large glazed conservatory at the back of the house, we enjoyed the benefits of a generous sized garden, enclosed by a six foot high brick wall. It was mostly laid to lawn with a concrete path on one side that led from the back door to the garage, situated at the end of the garden.

The path was set about a doors width from the wall, creating a border that was planted with a variety of herbs at the kitchen end, and gave way to several rose bushes, and mother's favourite summer flowers at the other.

Two very tall metal poles were sited adjacent to either end of the path, with a washing line suspended between them that was raised and lowered by means of pulleys and loops of waxed cord. Mother needed a long washing line and strong arms for her to keep up with the amount of washing created by four very active children, not to mention the daily requirement of work clothes for our father.

The annual six week school summer holiday had started and so far the weather had been very pleasant, allowing us to spend endless hours in the garden, or out with our friends using the play equipment at the local recreation ground.

My favourite item was the 'Witch's Hat'; an inverted cone of metal bars for climbing, pivoted on a central metal pole with a wooden board around the base, set about eighteen inches off the ground as a seat. I can remember times when ten to fifteen children, usually boys, clung fearlessly to the structure, like pirates on the rigging of some old galleon, using their body weight to make it gyrate wildly before leaping down to the surrounding tarmac. These were the days before soft play surfaces where bruised shins and grazed elbows were the boasting rights of a day's play.

On the morning in question, us three eldest, the youngest only being three, had decided to play in the garden, and had struggled to erect our small, white canvass, bivouac tent, ready to play it's part in whatever escapade we might dream up.
After a brief debate and a few tears from my sister, who was averse to playing Cowboys and Indians, yet AGAIN, it was decided that we should be doctors and nurses.

As the senior male, I would of course be the doctor (*I don't remember being aware of any female doctors at the time*) and she would be nurse, mostly because amongst her dressing up clothes she had a full nurses outfit, which she donned, complete with white cap and apron, each emblazoned with a red cross. There was also a stethoscope, which I quickly commandeered, strapping it around my neck.

Our younger brother, with no say in the matter, was nominated as the patient, to suffer all manner of illnesses and ailments and succumb to bandaging, splinting and the regular taking of his temperature, without complaint.

We had been playing for a while, our patient having endured the many privations of our make-believe cures for several previously unheard of diseases, which had been dreamt up by us as the medical team, when our attention was drawn to the squeaking of the wrought iron back gate as it opened.

I looked out from the tent in time to see a small female face appear tentatively around the corner of the garage. It was a friend of my sister, who wondered if she could join in our game. Having exhausted our sole patient to the point of fedupidness, we readily availed ourselves of the opportunity to extend the duration of our quackery, and invited her in.

Realising that it was not possible for the doctor and nurse to treat two patients at the same time in our small field hospital, I quickly adjusted the diagnosis of our younger brother to fully recovered, and dispatched him to the house to gain some refreshments for the new patient and us medicos. I then invited the new patient to take her place on the blanket in the tent, which she did willingly, ably assisted by the nurse.

Now comfortably settled in, it was time for me, the doctor, to examine the patient and determine what ailment afflicted her. First, the nurse vigorously shook the pretend plastic thermometer, on which the painted red line never moved, and carefully placed it under the patient's tongue.

Next, it was important for the doctor to listen to the patient's heart; well it's what always seemed to happen when we were taken to the real doctor for a check-up, and so the nurse dutifully unbuttoned her friend's blouse in readiness.

Now at this point I should probably explain that this all happened in the late 1950's, when children of both sexes wore vests both summer and winter, come rain or shine, without exception.

Placing the pretend stethoscope on the young lady's cotton covered chest, I, duty bound as the doctor, listened intently for a few seconds before announcing that it was beating, and therefore that couldn't possibly be the problem. My sister as the nurse then re-buttoned her friend's blouse and we, as the medical team, had a debate as to what rare disorder her friend could possibly be suffering from.

Our deliberations were interrupted when mother's legs appeared at the triangular aperture of the tent and further investigation revealed that she had arrived carrying a tray with three brightly coloured plastic beakers of orange juice, and an array of biscuits.

Obviously our other patient had decided that now he was cured, he no longer needed our attention and had found something else to occupy his time.

Mother asked if we were enjoying our game, to which we all gave an affirmative reply, whereupon she reminded us that father would be home for lunch in an hour or so, and when he got here we would have to stop playing, and our patient, who would no doubt be expected back at home for her lunch, would have to leave.

So later, when the squeaking of the gate signalled father's arrival, we said our goodbyes and headed indoors.

After lunch was over and father had returned to work, we children played in the back room, while mother busied herself with her never ending list of household chores. The phone rang in the living room and mother broke mid-task to answer it, closing the door behind her, which naturally fostered an inquisitive silence from us. At first there was no sound of conversation, then came the muted tones of questions being asked, followed by the timbre of an apology.

The living room door opened and mother, whose countenance bore the signs of both embarrassment and displeasure in equal measure, strode towards me, stopping abruptly at my side. She demanded that I stand and follow her to the kitchen, instructing the other children to stay where they were.

It transpired that it had been my sister's, friend's mother on the phone, who, having found her daughter's blouse wrongly buttoned, was extremely indignant that her clothes had been rearranged by me! Mother demanded to know what had occurred in the tent.

I explained that we had been playing doctors and nurses and that I had wanted to listen to the girl's heart, as any good doctor would, and it had been my sister who had undone and re-buttoned the blouse.

My protestations were to no avail as, being the oldest, I was reminded that the responsibility fell to me, and I was summarily dismissed to my bedroom to await my father's judgement of Solomon on his return.

Eventually things blew over and, later in the summer holidays, the girl's mother allowed her to play with us again, however, as you can see, the injustice of the incident has remained with me to this day.

GRANDDAD'S INVENTION

"I don't know!" said Arthur, as he walked into the lounge. It was a bright sunny day outside, however, the curtains had been drawn so that his two grandsons could better see the extremely lifelike avatars of football players, dashing about the green, perfectly manicured turf of the TV computer game.

"You two should be out in the garden, playing football for real, not in here straining your eyes to see the telly," Arthur continued.

"Shhh! Granddad," said Matthew, the elder by a year at nine, "Jacob's one up and I've only got seconds to get a goal."

"I'll give you Shhh!" replied Arthur, as he headed across the room and drew the curtains, banishing the gloom in favour of bright, warm sunshine.

"Oh Granddad!" came the almost instantaneous duet, followed quickly by a loud cheer from Jacob as he leapt to his feet, thrusting his arms in the air, his joy in beating his elder brother spread wide over his beaming face.

This provoked Matthew to dump his controller unceremoniously on the floor, and throw himself back onto the settee with his arms tightly folded across his chest, contorting his face into the sort of a grimace that could strip paint.

"Come on Matthew," said Arthur reproachfully "It's only a game."

"Hmmph!" was the best response that Matthew could muster, while Jacob, still relishing his victory, ran to the kitchen to apprise Grandma of his sporting prowess.

Arthur hadn't intended to put a dampener on his grandsons' fun, far from it in fact. His objective had been to motivate them into a more healthy, energetic activity, such as playing real football in the garden, or bouncing around on, what to his mind had been, a rather expensive trampoline that Joyce had persuaded him to buy, knowing that Matthew and Jacob would be spending a fair part of their school summer holiday with them. However, Arthur still wasn't sure if the origin of the persuading hadn't come from the boys themselves.

With Matthew, still attached limpet like to the settee, and Jacob giving a fully animated account of the game to Grandma, Arthur made his way to the back door, collecting a key from the row of cup hooks on the wall, the one marked 'SHED'.

"I'll be in the shed if anyone's looking for me," he called out to Joyce, who briefly broke eye contact with Jacob, and looked up at him with a knowing smile.

However, at hearing the word 'shed', Jacob's focus quickly changed, knowing full well that Grandad's 'shed' held all manner of exciting curiosities. "Can I come Granddad?"

A little surprised at his sudden return to popularity, Arthur replied "Of course Jacob."

"Off you go then," said Joyce, her voice showing no intonation of her grateful reprieve from Jacob's exuberant recountment of his victory over Matthew.

Arthur let Jacob go first, and they made their way across the lawn to the small, dark, timber building nestling next to the leylandii hedge.

Arthur wiggled the key into the well-worn keyhole and undid the padlock. He released the hasp from the staple and opened the shed door, the unoiled hinges squeaking with resentment.

As the door swung open, and they crossed the threshold, they were welcomed with the oddly, comforting aroma of warm creosote and the musty smell of old things.
Jacob's eyes were wide with anticipation, and Arthur found a wooden box for Jacob to stand on, and put next to his stool at the bench.

"Granddad, did you have a shed when you were a boy?" Jacob enquired.

"No!" chuckled Arthur, "But I did used to sneak into my Dad's shed when he was at work. That would be your Great Granddad Michael's shed."

"Wow!" retorted Jacob, "Have there always been sheds Granddad?"

"Probably," replied Arthur wistfully, "Well, ever since we men left the caves anyway," he said, smiling down at Jacob.

"What did you do in your Dad's shed?" asked Jacob, hoping that Grandad might expound on some illicit story that he could tell Matthew later.

"I used to make things with bits of timber and sometimes even invent things," Arthur said.

"Wow!" Jacob exclaimed once more.

The shed door creaked open and Matthew, who had no doubt been encouraged by his Grandma, stood silhouetted against the bright green of the sunlit lawn beyond and, having heard the tail end of the conversation asked "What did you invent Granddad?"

"Ooooo! Let me think now," replied Arthur as Matthew came and stood beside his brother "There were a few things, if only I can remember them. Hmmm! I did invent a digital bolt once, so that you could lock your garden gate."

"Can we see it," interrupted Jacob.

"Well no, it didn't actually get made Jacob," Arthur replied "but I did send the details of it off to Yale locks, I think I've still got the drawing of it somewhere, along with their reply" And with that Arthur turned to an old, steel, two draw, filing cabinet that stood on the floor against the rear wall of the shed. It supported a rolled up canvass something or other, which lay there like a huge, squashed, Swiss roll.

The venerable cabinet sported a glossless coat of battleship grey paint and patches of rust in equal measure, what some trendy folk these days might call 'shabby chic'. As he pulled open the bottom draw it emitted a high pitched squeal. Jacob squeezed his eyes shut, hunched his shoulders and put his fingers in his ears.

Similarly affected, Matthew exclaimed in a raised voice "I think that needs some oil

Granddad," feeling pleased with himself that he could offer advice to Arthur.

"It's not the only thing around here that needs oiling," grunted Arthur, bent over as he was, flicking through the files in the draw until he came to the one he was looking for. "Here it is," he said, with a note of accomplishment. He placed the folder on the bench and opened it, and the boys strained forward to see the contents.

"There we go," said Arthur, carefully opening a fragile folded piece of lined schoolbook notepaper to which was stapled a typed letter on headed paper with the words 'Yale Locks' emblazoned at the top.

This time Jacob let out a more elongated and lower pitched "Wowww!," as he scanned the details on the page.

Arthur flipped the letter over to the rear so that only the drawing was visible, and placed the documents back on the bench. The two sketches were in 2D and done in back biro, both had been shaded with cross hatching so that what the boys, and Arthur, were looking at were two cylinders.

The top one had a dome section at one end with what looked like the shaft of a slip bolt at the other. There were four numbered rings taking up most of the length of the cylinder, each one having a raised serrated edge. The lower drawing showed the same object but in two parts, with a toothed bar attached to the slip bolt part. "The top one shows it locked and the bottom one unlocked," Arthur said, pointing to each sketch in turn.

"How did you think it up?" enquired Matthew, with genuine interest.

"Well, back then we used to have security chains for our bikes with digital locks on, and I based my design on that."

"How did it work?" Jacob asked, not wanting to show any less interest than his elder sibling.

"You see the numbers?" asked Arthur, pointing to the top sketch.

"Yes!" they both replied.

"You made up your own code number, say 4609, and then, when you turned the wheels so that the numbers lined up, you could pull the slip bolt out, and unlock whatever it was you had locked up."
"Why didn't they make your bolt Granddad," asked Jacob, making sure that he got his question in first this time.

"I'll read you their letter, shall I?" Arthur answered, to which they both nodded.

Both the boys listened intently as Arthur flipped the letter back over and began to read. "Dear 'MR' Johnson – I felt very grown up, I can tell you, when I first read the letter," said Arthur, before continuing "Dear Mr Johnson, Thank you for the drawings of your proposed digital slip bolt. Our technical team have looked at them carefully, but find several weaknesses in your design, particularly with respect to the slenderness of the slip bolt key. We have therefore concluded that it is a not a project with which we can proceed. Thank you again for your interest. Yours faithfully and signed Mr E J Harris. General Manager."

"It's a shame they didn't use your design Granddad, you might have been rich by now," Matthew said, rather perceptively for his young age.

Arthur laughed out loud at the thought of it. "If only," he said, refolding the papers and returning the folder to the filing cabinet, before squeaking the draw shut again and, feeling that the earlier unhappy mood had now dissipated he said "Come on boys, that's enough about Granddad's invention, let's go and see if Grandma still has some of those choc-ice lollies in the freezer, and afterwards I'll watch you play on the trampoline."

Matthew and Jacob didn't need asking twice, and set off at a gallop, nearly reaching the back door by the time Arthur had managed to lock up the shed.

A WALK INTO PARADISE

"……………. yes, OK Mum – yes, I promise I'll phone Catherine later – yes, I remembered to send her a card – Mum, I'm going to be late for work – yes, it IS going to be a busy day, I'm moving offices – yes, because of the promotion – I've got to go Mum – yes, I'll phone you later to tell you how things went – OK Mum, must go, bye – yes Mum, bye for now – love you too – bye! – bye! – got to go! – bye!" and with that Peter put the cordless phone back in its cradle, firmly holding it in place for a few moments, as though willing it not to ring again.

"I know she means well, but she always manages to phone at inconvenient times," thought Peter, tipping his head to the ceiling in exasperation, audibly cracking the muscles in his neck. His anxiety levels were already at 'HIGH' alert, inexorably heading for 'SEVERE'.

He hadn't slept at all well the night before, from thinking about all the things that he had to do today. He must have mentally filled in and rewritten several check lists in his head, while staring despondently at the bedroom ceiling. "I don't know how she does it, I really don't; TODAY! of all days and …." quickly glancing at his watch "….. if I don't get a move on I'll miss the bus."

Peter quickly gathered the pile of papers off the table, shoving them haphazardly into his document case, managing to catch a rogue sheet mid-flight on its way to the floor. "I'll have to sort them on the bus," his thoughts now trying to race ahead of his actions.

He quickly grabbed the mug from the kitchen worktop and downed the much needed dregs of coffee with a slight grimace. "Better cold than not at all," he thought, placing the now empty cup into the sink and, even though his head was buzzing, he couldn't escape the image of his mother staring sternly, horrified at him leaving the house with dirty crocks in the sink. "I'll wash it later," he said out loud, as though trying to rebuff her unheard criticism.

Peter tucked the document case under his arm and headed for the front door, lifting and pocketing the house keys from the hall stand on the way. As he passed, he momentarily looked into the hall mirror and, with a slight nod, silently complimented himself on his turn out. "You'll do, considering the chaos," he thought and then, turning towards the door, he pushed up the snib of the night latch with his thumb and twisted the oval knob anticlockwise.

The shoot bolt withdrew from strike plate with its usual slight jolt, causing the letter plate to rattle. Peter opened the door wide and, as he stepped over the threshold onto the top step of three leading to the pavement, the sound and smells of the busy street inundated his senses, and he was bathed in warm morning sunlight. He breathed in deeply, partly releasing some of the pressure he felt bearing down on him. "At least it's a good day for it," he thought, as he turned and pulled the door shut, giving it a quick push with the flat of his hand, to make sure that it had locked tight.

Unfortunately, Peter's level of stress quickly re-established its upward trajectory, as he became aware of the deep growl of a bus's heavy diesel engine. Still facing the door, he quickly looked over his left shoulder; his eyes widened and his jaw slackened, as sure enough, above next doors hedge, he could see a large red double decker heading in his direction, boldly brandishing the number 42, and sailing like a stately ship in a sea of traffic, flowing relentlessly towards the city. He could hear that it was already slowing for the bus stop, which was still a couple of hundred yards dash for him along the pavement to his right.

Panicked into action he turned, and in one bound leapt the three steps to the street below, however, because of the height of the hedge, he hadn't seen the cyclist pedalling for all he was worth along the pavement, illegally using it as a cycle lane to try and beat the more sluggish flow of traffic.

"Watch out you idiot" the cyclist screamed.

Startled by the shout, Peter turned, just in time to see his black Lycra clad assassin, wearing a yellow and black striped cycle helmet, looking for all the world like a giant hornet, bearing down on him at speed. With fear rooting Peter to the spot, a painful impact was inevitable.

"Well! That's buggered that then," thought Peter, as he looked around trying to get his bearings, in what seemed to be an endless black void.

To be sure there had been some pain at his passing, he distinctly remembered how the front bike tyre had rolled up the side of his right leg, cracking the cruciate ligament and snapping the femur, which made the wheel buckle. Then, as the bike spun on its front forks, the handle bars, still bearing the weight of the now airborne cyclist, had entered his chest, breaking several ribs forcing the air out of his now punctured lung.

"That bit must have been gory for the passing bus passengers to witness," he thought.

Then finally, as Peter fell, the bike, still continuing on its radial trajectory, caused the spinning rear wheel to cut like a bacon-slicer into the right side of his neck, severing his carotid artery.

"No! Thinking about it that would have been gorier," he rectified, although, remembering the last conscious view of the world now lost to him, which was of a super-sized hornet tumbling along the pavement, before being squashed under the rear wheels of the number 42 bus.

"Actually, that was probably the goriest," Peter thought, with a grimace.

"I'm not sure what's supposed to happen next," Peter pondered. He had read that sometimes patients in hospital, who had theoretically died on the operating table, had reported out of body experiences on their recovery. Indeed, stories abounded of a light that you were supposed to walk into but, although he was sure that he was looking, he couldn't actually see anything, not even himself come to that, let alone walk anywhere.

Peter sensed that it was highly unlikely he would be taking a walk into paradise through the fabled 'Pearly Gates' anytime soon.

"Oh damn!" he thought suddenly "I left the dirty coffee cup in the sink!" which, as it turned out, was the last thought Peter ever experienced.

……….. and FINALLY

If the human race maintains reproduction levels at their current rate, which by default of habitation will continue to strip the world of its green canopy; and if CO_2 emissions are not curtailed, leading to an increase in global temperatures, and the warming and acidification of the oceans, which will decimate the phytoplankton; where will our oxygen come from?

….. and what will happen to us when they find micro plastics in raindrops?

Printed in Poland
by Amazon Fulfillment
Poland Sp. z o.o., Wrocła